FRIENDS LIKE THAT

Also by Alexandria Blaelock

FICTION
That Love Nonsense
Taipan vs Brown
The Ghost and Ms Cox

SHORT STORY COLLECTIONS
The Haunting of Hayward Hall
Lovelorn, Lovestruck and Love at First Sight
Common or Garden Variety Heroes
Case Files of the Wilkinson National Detective Agency
Unavoidable Fates
Christmas Travesties
Five Faces of Felicia Clarke
Little Place Called Home

MS BLAELOCK'S BOOKS
Stress Free Dinner Parties
Signature Wardrobe Planning
Holistic Personal Finance
Minimally Viable Housekeeping
Planning a Life Worth Living

SELECTED SHORT STORIES
Alma's Grace
Balancing the Book
Bygone Boyfriend
Christmas Bonanza
Fate in Your Hands
Kiss of Death
Lady of the Looking Glass
Love in the Security Directorate
Morning Star, Evening Star, Superstar
Needy Bitch
Payton's Run
Secret Singer
Shining Star
Ship in a Bottle
The Shadow Thieves
The Palace Hotel
The Pseudonym's Bride

FRIENDS LIKE THAT

A SHORT NOVEL

ALEXANDRIA BLAELOCK

BlueMere Books
MELBOURNE, AUSTRALIA

For permission requests, please contact
enquiries@bluemerebooks.com.

Ordering Information:
Discounts are available on quantity purchases. For details, contact
orders@bluemerebooks.com.

Friends Like That/Alexandria Blaelock
hardback ISBN: 978-1-922744-56-2
paperback ISBN: 978-1-922744-57-9
digital ISBN: 978-1-922744-58-6
AI generated audio: 978-1-922744-59-3

Book Layout © BookDesignTemplates.com
Cover Art © stokkete/Depositphotos

For all who miss their loved ones.

Having a place to go is a home.
Having someone to love is a family.
Having both is a blessing.

– DONNA HEDGES

It was an ordinary day. So perfectly ordinary that most people take them for granted.

There's nothing particularly dreadful or delightful about an ordinary day. They're just the days that don't make it into your long-term memory if you're not the type of person who regularly keeps a diary.

The morning was not too hot and not too cold. The breeze neither too rough nor too gentle.

The sun, however, was warm enough to rest comfortably on Ellie Porterfield's back, but not so warm she felt a need to take her sky blue cashmere overcoat off.

It was a day like thousands before it, the sort of day Ellie also took for granted.

And it was also the manner of day she would come to long for.

Ellie worked at the Porterfield Department Store.

So far as she knew, she was no relation to THE Porterfields who started the store in 1892.

Her mother had burned up in a nightclub fire when she was five, presumably with her father, though she had no recollection of him.

She could, however, remember the scratchy black suit the man who left her in the orphanage was wearing. The way it felt as she held his arm, begging him not to leave her there.

The way it felt as he wrenched it free of her grip, and the hardness of the tiled floor as she fell to her knees and watched him walk away.

Not looking back even once.

Perhaps because of a succession of unpleasant stints in a long chain of foster homes and care facilities, she blocked the memories of what she assumed was the happiest time of her life that came before.

About all she remembered of her mother was blonde hair piled on the top of her head in an intriguing series of curls, along with the smell of sweat and sandalwood.

As she grew older, she fantasised, not of being a Princess, but of being a Porterfield.

That the Porterfields would swoop in and rescue her. Dress her in clothes worthy of the department store's windows and feed her food more delicious and more plentiful than she could imagine.

By the time she turned eighteen and found herself outside the last care facility's door, clutching a single black plastic bag containing significantly less than what she considered her property, she understood at last she was not a long-lost heiress.

If the Porterfields hadn't claimed her by now, she simply wasn't related. She was on her own, and would have to fight and work hard to achieve everything she wanted in life.

Given her parents were dead and twenty years had passed since their demise, there seemed little chance of finding out for sure who her parents were now.

Or, to be honest, much point.

In any case, she'd interviewed for a general women's department sales position at the Porterfield Department Store. Not because she fostered any hope of being claimed by them, but because it was the only place she could think of. But, they placed her in the exclusive high-end fashion department instead.

So exclusive you had to book an appointment and take a private lift to the swipe card protected top floor.

The show room was lit with a soft, kind to wrinkles glow, in which several brightly spotlighted mannequins featured the latest designs.

On receiving notification a customer had arrived, Ellie would escort her female, or somewhat more discretely male, client to the floor. Usher them into a spacious changing room and draw the sumptuous rose gold satin curtains closed behind them.

She'd invite them to sit on a matching velvet Chippendale style chair and lay their bags on a short, wide black lacquered chest of drawers packed with pins, tape measures and other assorted items needed to ensure the correct fit.

Taking a small, refrigerated bottle of sparkling mineral water from the cut crystal tray on the drawers, she'd half fill a matching glass and settle it within easy reach of the chair.

She'd stand before her wealthy customer, hands clasped in front of her and head respectfully bowed as they sipped their water and discussed what kind of garment and occasions they were looking for.

Then leave them alone with the muted sound of classic orchestral music, carefully drawing the curtains back across the changing room to ensure privacy while they disrobed.

In the meantime, she collected together a small selection of suitable clothing on a wheeled rack and brought it back to the changing room.

If they needed a little nip and tuck to ensure the correct fit, Ellie pinned out the garments and whisked them away to a carefully concealed and sound proofed room of sewing machinists.

She'd invite them to take a beauty treatment or have their hair styled in the adjoining luxury salon while they waited.

Or perhaps they'd take a little lunch or an apéritif in the exclusive and mind-numbingly expensive café on the same floor

Away from the common people.

So while Ellie didn't know who her parents were, given that the department store called her Miss Porterfield, sent her to the elite salon where they handed her all the difficult customers, she was fairly certain it was because of her name.

Perhaps her exclusive clientele imagined she was learning the roped from the ground up. And perhaps they treated her with a modicum of respect because of that.

But, as Porterfield had an excellent employee discount program, and she was required to wear more sophisticated clothing, she was not about to complain.

What Ellie didn't know was the years of living in care had given her abilities so precious few people ever master them.

Including the ability to sit quietly and unobtrusively, barely noticed by those not looking specifically for her. To keep her thoughts to herself, not showing them on her face, nor gossiping about them.

But, with her long black hair and strikingly handsome square face, dressed in her expensive clothes, there was a bonus. People were in awe of her, a little afraid of her, and often scared to think about approaching her.

Also, thanks to her early years, she lived a self-contained life, rarely impacting on others. No real friends, just larger-than-life characters from movies and television shows who walked, in her imagination, by her side.

Ellie lived in a tiny studio apartment in an outer suburb of Melbourne.

In a former life, the building had been a large, imposing, private house. Developers swept up the derelict house and converted it into an apartment building.

Thanks to the bus and train ride required to get to the city, the rent was cheap, despite the beauty of the building's façade and period features.

So cheap Ellie could afford it because despite the generous employee discount, or perhaps because of it, Porterfield doesn't pay much.

And so we find her at the bus stop, on her way to work, on this unremarkable Autumn day.

The stop sits on the edge of a four-lane highway lined with small shops and offices.

Ellie walks an extra fifteen minutes to reach this stop because more buses going to the train station stop there than the one closer to the studio attic apartment she calls home.

She waited patiently, make-up as immaculate as you'd expect from someone using (discounted) luxury skincare.

Under her overcoat, she wore a short-sleeved fitted real silk dress with an abstract red, blue and yellow pattern that reminded her of stained glass windows.

And incredibly soft and comfortable low-heeled black shoes that are well out of most people's price range.

The air was still, the cold biting pleasantly in her face, and the reason she wore the soft, warm overcoat with its handy, deep pockets too.

Plus, the lightweight black and white paisley merino scarf wound around her neck and tucked under the coat collar. Where it partly covered her chest and kept out the chill.

And to top it, a small, soft black shoulder bag from the company that produced the shoes.

Her black sunglasses had gold coloured lenses that literally coated everything she saw with sunshine.

As she waited for the bus, she listened to the latest episode of her favourite mystery podcast with her wireless ear buds. Her phone and hands thrust deep into her pockets.

It was never her attention to stand alone at one end of the bus stop while everyone else stood at the other, but her well-dressed appearance and expressionless face were enough to make them nervously stand well back of her.

Even though they have seen her in exactly the same place, at exactly the same time, every single working day for as long as any of them can remember.

Ellie had not slept well.

The property agent had informed her the rent was going up, and she'd spent most of the night lying awake, trying to work out how to pay for it.

So unfair.

It was looking a lot like she might have to move even further out.

Or worse, get a new job.

Despite the difficult customers, she loved her job, and the luxuries she could afford because of it.

She closed her eyes and turned her face to the sun, hoping for a recharge.

So, she didn't notice the man with blood dripping down his face as he staggered towards the bus stop.

Nor hear her fellow passengers whispered comments and speculation.

Was completely oblivious when they sidled away from him like a flock of starlings as he reeled by the stop.

As if his target was the flawlessly dressed woman.

The man reached toward her, grabbing her precious coat as he fell, pulling her down on top of him.

She saw him say, "help me," before he passed out.

She looked around for help, seeing the other people at the busstop take a few steps back

Ellie, took an ear bud out so she could hear what they were saying.

A man reaching into his pocket grimaced, shook his head and retreated a little further.

Ellie, bit her lip, perplexed.

Admittedly, a man literally falling at her feet was unusual, but she'd expected a little more help.

She didn't want to get involved either, but looking down at him, she really had no choice, and not knowing exactly what to do, fell back on her First Aid training.

Porterfield didn't want any of their VIP customers actually dying in store, so like the other high-end departmental staff, Ellie was a trained First Aid officer.

Though Porterfield's concern only extended to their business premises; no matter how important a customer was, once they'd left, they were someone else's problem.

Ellie sat up and spoke to the man, "Sir, are you all right? "Sir?"

The man did not answer, so she shook him a little.

Hopefully, enough to rouse him sufficiently to pass the responsibility onto someone else, but not enough to do any further damage, "Sir?"

Shook him a little harder, "Sir?"

Kneeling on the pavement, damaging her tights even more than they already were, she checked his body for visible wounds.

The head wound would be enough for a concussion, but his skull didn't seem to be fractured, so that was lucky for him. As was the lack of obvious blood from other areas, though, who knew what was going on inside his body?

He was still breathing, so she gently rolled him into the recovery position, absently noting the cheap fabric of his black suit under her fingers, before she called an ambulance.

Her coat would, of course, need to be cleaned.

But if the ambulance came quickly, she might still get to work in time for her first appointment.

Sadly, luck was not on her side that morning.

Aside from a man blundering into her, a bus arrived before the ambulance. And she couldn't, in good conscience, get into it, leaving the man alone and unconscious by the side of the road.

Reluctantly, she waved the bus on and waited some more.

It was peak hour, and the traffic looked monstrous.

She'd watched a news article on the television the night before about the long ambulance call times in the outer suburbs getting up to ten minutes. Or even longer. One cited case twenty-four minutes!

She let another bus go by and reluctantly called into work.

Luckily, she lived so far out of the City it was still relatively early, and no one was there, so she left a message.

"This is Ellie Porterfield," she said, the tone sounding higher in her ears, and the words pouring from her mouth faster than her usual measured pace, "I'm with an injured man waiting for an ambulance. I'm not sure when I'll get in, but I'll definitely be late for my first appointment. Possibly the second as well."

Even as the words left her mouth, she wondered if she'd said too many of them. If something about the stress of the situation made her chattier than usual.

With the call taken care of, she turned her attention back to the man.

Still breathing.

And, as she smoothed his short black hair away from his unshaven triangular shaped face, still bleeding.

And a handful of tissues wouldn't be much help.

Sighing, she unwound the scarf from her neck, pausing regretfully for a second or two before using it to apply additional pressure to the wound.

Making a mental note to buy, and carry, some large handkerchiefs from the menswear department for future emergency situations.

At last she heard the wail of sirens, saw flashing lights and the traffic moving as far as the drivers could over to the edges of the road to make space.

The ambulance inched its way through and pulled over into the bus lane next to the stop.

A female ambulance officer leapt out and ran across the pavement towards her, while a man grabbed a gurney and a big black bag from the back.

"What's happened here?" the woman asked.

"I don't know. He just turned up and grabbed me as he fell."

The male officer arrived with the gurney and checked the injured man over.

"Do you know his name, or anything about him?" the woman asked.

Ellie watched as the other ambulance officer threw her scarf to the side and applied some bandages to the injured man's head.

"No. He didn't tell me, and I didn't check his pockets for a wallet."

The officer seemed satisfied with that, and turning to her partner, relayed the information as they got him onto the gurney and into the ambulance almost before Ellie had drawn breath.

Her services were no longer required.

She picked up her bloodstained scarf, free to continue her day, and yet she hesitated.

Should she go to the hospital with him?

It wasn't as if she knew him. Or really cared whether some low life criminal was okay.

But there was something about the cheapness of his suit that roused her pity.

Assuming the negative, the officers slammed the ambulance doors, one running around to the driver's side and it left; sirens blaring and lights flashing as it zoomed away.

3

The next bus worth of people at the stop left Ellie and her bloodstained clothes alone for a different reason.

By the time she arrived at work, having replayed the events over and over all the way in, Ellie was in shock herself.

Muscles weak, chest tight, and a cold heaviness in her guts.

Stumbling as she bought and immediately drank half a strong, sweet milky coffee.

Leaning on the counter for support as she dropped the coat and scarf in at the ground floor dry cleaner.

Rubbing her eyes and face as she waited for the discrete elevator, letting it return to the top floor before recollecting herself and calling it back again.

Not having any idea how she was going to get through the rest of the day.

Obviously, everyone wanted to know what had happened and made her repeat the story seemingly endlessly.

And as more people heard what had happened, she heard them repeating it to others, and as the tale passed from person to person, it got larger and larger until it took on a life of its own.

And as the story grew, she became more and more uncomfortable in her own skin.

Staff from the lower floors were sneaking up to the strictly off-limits top floor to get the story from the horse's mouth herself.

Eventually, her voice just stopped working altogether.

Her boss, Mrs Mainwaring, called Ellie into her office and closed the door.

She walked to sit behind the desk

"What have you to say for yourself?" she snapped.

Ellie, standing head bowed before the desk, in the same submissive pose she used with customers, said nothing.

"What did you think you were doing? You've turned the High End Fashion department into a circus. Take a couple of days off to have a long, hard look at yourself. Don't come back until Monday."

Ellie nodded and turned away.

Staff members skittered away like mice when she opened the office door.

Once she'd closed the door behind her, she took a deep breath and sighed it out.

She was fairly sure Mrs Mainwaring was shouting for the sake of the eavesdroppers. Also fairly sure the woman had meant the time off as a kind gesture.

But early Friday afternoon, when she wasn't working over the weekend, was not as generous as it could have been.

Less generous also, because the trains at that time of day stopped all stations instead of express. Plus, she had to wait longer than usual for both the train and the bus, and had to deal with the private school children commuting at the same time. It was almost more than she could bear on the way home.

She grabbed her bag, bought the handkerchiefs, collected her dry cleaning, and took the train and a bus back home.

4

Arriving home not much earlier than usual, after what seemed like a lifetime away, Ellie was suspicious and annoyed to find her front door ajar when she knew perfectly well she'd locked it when she left.

She felt the blood drain from her face and unknowingly dropped into the fighting stance she'd learned while in care.

Her first assumption was the property agent had pre-empted her move by calling someone in to pack for her. It didn't occur to her it could be burglary, as she owned nothing of any value.

Not that she had any reason to suspect an eviction; she paid her rent in full on time every month, and as she always transferred directly to the agent's bank account, she could produce receipts to document the exact date and time of each payment.

And it wasn't as if she had any reason to suspect unacceptable behaviour on the agent's part, as they'd always left her to the quiet "enjoyment" of the apartment as they were required to by law.

But it was because the threat of eviction loomed large in her imagination; she could see herself kicking and screaming as thugs extracted her and all her possessions from the apartment to the street.

Logically, as soon as she got through the shock and grief stage to the planning stage, her rent would still get paid, even if she had to scrimp a little further.

Or, if the worse came to the worse, manage by dipping into her savings.

It's just that given her background, the worse case scenario was always the first thing she thought of.

After all, it had happened to her before.

Regardless, with the idea of a breaking and entering property agent firmly lodged in her brain, she was prepared for a fight by the time she slammed the door open and released a torrent of invective at the agent.

She slowed down, reduced the volume and finally stopped talking when her brain registered what her eyes were seeing.

Her jaw dropped.

She was looking at a crime scene.

Or a paranormal event.

Overturned and smashed furniture. Every drawer in the place emptied on the floor. Curtains ripped from the rails.

The amount of broken crockery and glassware suggested someone had organised a Greek dinner party while she was out, and not invited her.

On top of everything else that had happened, she was turning to double check she was in the right apartment when something moved, or fell, in the kitchenette, where she couldn't see it.

Unnerved, she quietly closed the door and as she started walking back down the stairs, called the Police.

After a brief wait, a man answered, "this is Constable Matias. How can I help you?"

"I just got home, and someone's broken in and trashed the place."

"As far as you know, is there anything missing?"

"I can't tell. It pretty much looks like a bomb site, but I think I disturbed the burglar."

"Okay, I'll send a unit out. Don't go inside and don't touch anything."

Ellie walked back to the main road, and a little further, until she came to the closest café where she ordered the largest cup of tea possible.

And went to the bathroom while she waited.

Started drinking it as she retraced her steps back home.

Hoping whoever had broken in had cleared out by now.

Steeling herself, she opened the door and looked in.

Taking a long, hard look around.

Her apartment was one of four tiny attic apartments. Not as bad as it could have been because they'd insulated it before they lined it, and rented out. But without air-conditioning or apartments above her, still hot in summer and cold in winter.

The door opened to the left, normally revealing an expanse of white walls and grey carpets, ending at a large gable containing two casement windows.

Theoretically, the windows were a fire escape, but also added headroom and brought light into the attic, where the white walls could reflect it around the room.

It was about as bad as she was expecting it to be. She fought hard to resist the temptation to go in and start setting it to rights.

The bathroom was to the right as you opened the front door, its door a little further in. Usually it revealed a neat white tiled room with a white china hand basin opposite the door and a combined front loading washer and dryer wedged underneath it. A collapsible laundry basket wedged between the machine and the small glass doored shower on the right. The bathroom door hid the white toilet which faced the shower box.

Now as she looked at it, she could see her cosmetic and skincare containers scooped and squeezed out, and flung around the room along with the towels and laundry detergent.

The bathroom wall had a small white kitchenette lined up behind it, where it wasn't visible from the front door. It contained a sink, oven, small cook plate, a tiny fridge, and storage. But from that point of view, she saw cupboard contents strewn across the floor.

She'd salvaged an old pine dresser from a street dump, painted it white and used it to store her folding clothes. Its usual place was along the dividing kitchen/bathroom wall, almost disappearing into it, and she saw the drawers and contents scattered randomly as well.

And it seemed for no reason they'd pulled the white crystal bead curtain that gave the bed a little privacy from the door down.

Her hanging clothes usually hung from a plain white clothes rack set between the wall behind the door and the bed, now haphazardly thrown on the floor, making her wince.

Lord knew where the small coffee table she ate from while sitting on the bed was in the mess. Though she thought she saw the white painted shelves the television usually sat on.

She'd watched enough crime shows to think she knew they'd need to get the forensics out.

Though, would they really?

She wasn't so important they needed to look like they were doing something concrete when the Chief Commissioner rang to bust their balls.

Did they really do that anyway? Surely the Chief Commissioner'd be too busy dealing with the Police Minister's office.

She'd seen him on television, opening new Police Centres, announcing investigation or enforcement outcomes, and he didn't seem the type to get bogged down into the details of someone else's investigation.

Laughing as she imagined him calling the local station demanding to know where they were up to on her case.

And then the Police arrived.

Bad timing.

The man gave her a weird look, but woman looked more sympathetic.

"I'm Constable Peterson," he introduced himself, "and this is Constable Kirkpatrick. What seems to be the problem?"

Ellie gestured through the door, "I just got home, saw this, and thought I heard someone in the kitchenette."

"Wait here," he said, and looking carefully around him, walked past the bathroom to the kitchenette.

"All clear," he said, and Ellie swallowed to stop herself throwing up with relief.

He looked around himself again as he took a few steps back to the door, "anything valuable missing?"

"Constable Matias told me to wait outside, so I don't know. But I don't own anything valuable, and the volume of pieces suggests it's all there."

This time Constable Kirkpatrick looked at her weirdly, and Ellie shrugged.

Peterson checked the lock mechanism on the door, "it's broken so I recommend you get a locksmith to change the locks in case they come back."

"The property agent..." she waved her arms around, trying to suggest changing the locks wouldn't be that easy.

"You need to call the agent - they're required by law to attend to it immediately. If they don't, you can do it yourself, as long as you've attempted to let them know. If you keep the receipt, they have to pay you back within seven days."

Ellie felt her shoulders drop and nodded with relief.

Kirkpatrick wrote something on a card and handed it over. "This is your Police report number. Start cleaning, work out what's missing and let us know. We'll fill in the details and print out a copy for the insurance claim."

Ellie stuffed it in her bag, "you don't need crime scene investigators?"

The ghost of a smile crossed Peterson's face, "not if nothing of value has been taken."

Ellie nodded again, "well, thanks for coming."

As the officers descended the stairs, Ellie heard Peterson say something to Kirkpatrick that made her laugh.

And immediately assumed they were talking about her.

5

Ellie stepped inside the apartment and shut the door, slipped her shoes off in their usual spot, and quietly had a tantrum.

Bunching her fists, screaming with her lips tightly sealed, punching the air as she twisted back and forth on the spot.

Then grabbed her phone and, while still annoyed, dialled the property agent.

Who didn't answer.

She left a message, "someone has broken in and trashed my place. I urgently need a new lock on the door. If you don't return my call within an hour, I will call a locksmith and send you the bill."

Then hung up.

Relieved the call was over, but worried the tiniest bit, she sounded like a bitch. Though it hadn't occurred to her, the burglar might come back until the police officer mentioned it.

The prospect was concerning.

How, aside from changing the lock, would she be able to protect herself and her place?

Being five stories about the ground wasn't much of a defence when she'd watched movies featuring hair-raising chases from window to window of heritage buildings.

Not that there was anything she could do to either the exterior or interior, seeing as she was renting.

She squared her shoulders.

It was a necessary repair, and Ellie wanted it done immediately. Preferably before the burglary took even place.

While she doubted locksmiths' ability to time-travel, she could at least prevent the next break in.

For the moment, a change of clothes was required, but as she picked through the wreckage, looking for a coat hanger to hang her coat on the hook by the door, the enormity of it hit her.

It looked like someone had pulled her carefully laundered and folded clothes from the dresser, one by one, and thrown them around the room. Followed by the drawers. Then ripped her beautiful, expensive dresses from the hanging rail and tossed them on the top.

And the pièce de résistance, upended the bed on top of the lot.

She slumped to the edge of the bed and cried.

Great, gut-wrenching sobs that threw her to her knees, cradling her stomach.

Which made her retch.

Scrambled as fast as she could to the toilet, and threw up the tea.

Why did everything have to be so hard?

Resting her forehead on the rim of the bowl, yearning for a different life. With parents, friends, and a boyfriend who loved her.

The style of life where you got an education, had somewhere secure to live and things like this where just a blip that didn't turn your life from bad to abysmal.

But...

If wishes were horses, beggars would ride.

Her life was what it was. And it would not change if she remained kneelong on the cold bathroom tiles.

She pulled herself up, rinsed her mouth out and splashed cold water on her face. Her white face looked back at her from the newly cracked mirror.

She picked up a towel half smeared with cosmetics, found an almost "clean" patch and dried her face.

With no one to rely on but herself, it was time to make a plan.

Cleaning the small bathroom would give her somewhere clean to store salvageable items, so that would be the first thing to do.

Just in case they'd done something to the washing machine, she programmed a hot wash and pushed the start button.

Then looked around the apartment for some track pants, a t-shirt and a fleece.

Grimacing as she put them on, trying not to think of the man who had dropped them to the floor or what else he might have done with them. Or what the dirty old man or horny teenager might look like.

Because what woman would leave such a mess in her wake?

Ellie decided her thoughts were too loud in the quiet apartment. and turned her phone on to a podcast and turned the volume up.

Then cleaned the bathroom.

Scooped up the liquid and semi-solid with her washcloth.

Found her stick vacuum and vacuumed up up the powders.

Made up a dilute bleach solution in the sink and cleaned the toilet and shower cubicle.

The eye watering smell of bleach got up her nose, eliminating all traces of any aromas the burglar might have left behind.

Threw her toothbrush in the small bin and put it outside the bathroom door.

Got the spray mop out and did the floor.

Decided it was too noisy, and swapped to a lower volume of randomised music playback.

Put her hanging rail outside the bathroom behind the apartment door, and started picking up and hanging or folding her clothes.

They would, of course, all need washing.

Also thoroughly.

Scrupulously.

Though at least the freshly dry cleaned coat wouldn't need doing again.

Her eyes watered, but she blinked back the tears.

Blaming the bleach and not the trauma for the feelings of anger, helplessness, and resentment.

One thing at a time.

Get her apartment back into some kind of order.

Then think about how much it would cost to replace everything, because, of course, she didn't have any insurance.

And as a side issue, whether her brain would let her comfortably stay in the apartment. Could she let the incident go, or would she always wonder when the burglar would be back?

Then again, where exactly did she think she was going to go instead?

Circling back to the rent increase, a room in a share house?

She laughed derisively at herself, blinking back the tears once more.

But at least she'd cleaned the bathroom and sorted through her clothes.

The small patch of order amongst the chaos cheered her on. "You can do it!" her neatly stacked clothes seemed to say.

Got the slightly bigger bin from the kitchen; transferred the contents, cleaned the smaller bin, and left it in the bathroom.

Lugged the bigger one out into the bedroom.

Looking back to the bathroom with no small satisfaction, Ellie thought maybe she could do it.

But maybe not with the music.

In the blessed silence, she cleaned the drawers and put them back in the dresser.

Realised she couldn't salvage the bead curtain, so folded the wood, wrapped the beads around it and dropped it in the kitchen bin.

Then wrapped broken pieces of china in the sandalwood scented drawer liners as she picked them both off the floor and put them in the bin as well.

Tying a knot in the bag when it got full, replacing the liner, and leaving the full bag by the door to take out later.

Found her cheap alarm clock, plugged it back in and set it to the correct time.

It looked okay, but she hoped all the little lights that made up the numbers still worked.

Gave the tightly looped carpet a once over before attempting to right her cheap folding futon sofa bed; the frame seemingly stronger than she'd thought.

Mattress, sheets and quilt seemingly unstained, but the burglar had torn the pillows open and pulled the polyester stuffing out.

Why the pillows, but not the quilt? Or the mattress, for that matter?

Crammed the pillows in another bin bag and left them by the door.

Took the quilt out of its cover, opened the windows, and hung it over the windowsill.

Something she was not supposed to do, but did anyway on warm sunny days anyway to air it out.

Taking a moment to look out over the sunset lit suburbs, listening to the traffic and bird song, smelling someone else's Indian curry dinner.

Then back to business.

Folded the sheets and quilt cover, putting them in the bathroom with the rest of the washing to be done.

And that was half the place cleaned.

She checked her phone - no sign the agent had heard her message. Should she have texted as well?

"Apartment burgled," she texted before she could talk herself out of it, "need locksmith NOW."

Hoping, despite her experiences with them, they'd arrange everything and call her back. Set an alarm to go off in an hour, in case they didn't.

Put the kitchenette drawers back in their slots.

Cleaned the sink and counter with a spray, then filled the sink with soapy water in case there was anything undamaged left on the floor.

Started vacuuming the half eaten box of cereal, ground coffee and assorted dried goods off the floor.

What kind of person throws food all over the floor?

Were they just trashing the place, or looking for something? In television shows, it was usually cash, jewellery, or thumb drives.

None of which she had. Was it possible they had the wrong house?

Tried not to think too hard about what else it could be as she picked up more pieces, wrapped them in drawer liner or food wrappers and put them in the bin.

Righted the shelves, stacked her few books in them, picked up the television, plugged it in, turned it on to check if it still worked.

It did not.

Her lip quivered, but she sighed and clamped down on it, then transferred the television to the growing pile of rubbish by the door.

Emptied the vacuum into the bin, changed the bin liner and left another full one by the door.

Looked in the cupboards, then wondered why they'd left spilled food in there and not thrown it on the floor with the rest.

Put the open and damaged packages in the bin and changed the bin liner again.

Vacuumed the cupboards.

Emptied the vacuum.

Vacuumed some more cupboard.

Emptied the vacuum.

Minutely inspected her canned goods as she stacked them on the counter. Wiped the cupboard shelves down before wiping and returning the cans.

Wiped the tiny fridge out and discarded all the open containers, though at least there weren't many of them.

Soaked up the spills from the carpet with towels and vacuumed around them as she did the rest of it.

Deeply appreciating such a tiny apartment hadn't taken that long to clean.

The odd thing, though, was that the more she'd cleaned, the larger her sense of ownership over the space had become.

If a tidy desk equals a tidy mind, then an uncluttered clean and tidy apartment must equal a tidy brain.

She'd started cleaning with the idea that at least there would be less to move out with, and ended it with the opinion it would take more than a rent rise and a burglary to drive her out.

She called an emergency locksmith.

While she waited for them to arrive, she ferried all the rubbish down the stairs to the bin enclosure.

6

As it turned out, the lock on the door wasn't actually an external door lock.

Nor was the door or the frame suitable for external doors.

All it would take would be a good kick with a heavy boot, and the door would explode into splinters.

Understanding the attic conversion you live in is not the secure home you thought it was, is not the best news when you've come home to find yourself burgled.

Even if, as a technicality, nothing was actually stolen.

Ellie asked the locksmith to note his recommendation to replace the door on the invoice.

And paid the bill.

Left on her own again, she wasn't sure what to do next.

Go to bed, start washing her clothes, or go shopping.

But the local shopping centre was open late on Fridays, and there was a small Porterfield store in it.

So, she could at least get new pillows for the night.

And replace the crockery, glassware and groceries she'd just thrown out.

Perhaps something was finally going her way.

She decided not to change back into the mostly clean dress she'd worn that day, or some other possibly contaminated clothes from the apartment floor.

Just grabbed her bag, shoved her feet into some shoes, got her coat on and started walking.

But as she walked to the shops, she was miserable in what she saw as her déshabillé condition, no matter how reasonable the excuse was .

Everyone seemed to look quizzically at her casual clothing and formal overcoat, making her feel both under and overdressed at the same time.

Embarrassed as she was by her clothes, she didn't regret her decision to wear them, boldly returning glances in her direction.

Deciding housewares first, she shopped first for bedding and pillows. She wasn't fond of wearing or sleeping in clothes or linens without washing them first, but better that than the potentially contaminated sheets she owned.

She asked the Porterfield sales assistant, whose name tag proudly stated she was Sien, "would you please hold these for collection in an hour or so?"

"Of course. From here or from the collection point."

Ellie thought quickly and decided to take a taxi back with her shopping, "from the collection point please."

As she rooted through her shoulder bag to find her wallet, she found a small metallic thing that wasn't hers.

Not really looking at it, assuming it was rubbish she'd picked up in the apartment, she transferred it to her track pant pocket to throw it in a bin later. Then handed her staff discount and credit cards to Sien.

The woman glanced at the staff identification card, before narrowing her eyes and looking up at Ellie.

Coming to a decision, she asked, "are you aware you are wearing two different shoes?"

Ellie looked down to see a flat, black boot and a red loafer and laughed with relief.

So that was what it had all been about.

"I was not," she said, "but thank you for pointing it out."

Surprisingly, she did not feel compelled to offer an explanation. A new feeling, at odds with the pre-burglary Ellie.

She took the cards back and was just about to shove her wallet back in her bag when someone ran past her, taking it off her shoulder and running away with it down an escalator.

She grabbed her suddenly sore shoulder to soothe it, trying to work out what had happened before the realisation dawned.

"Hey!" she shouted, and chased after her bag.

Too late to see which way the person went when they exited the escalator.

Was it something to do with the metallic thing she'd just found in it?

She took it out of her pocket and saw a tiny flash drive. Not that she'd ever used one, but theoretically, she knew what it was.

When she went for her phone, she realised it was still in her bag. The one that was goodness knows where by now.

As was the card with Officer Kirkpatrick's number, the person she'd intended to call with the phone.

As well as the new key to the new deadlock on her door.

She sighed.

The streak of good luck was not so much a streak as a feint.

Putting the drive back in her track pants where it seemed to burn a hole in the pocket, she returned to complete her purchase.

"I've reported the theft of your bag to security," Sien said, "if we find it in the store we'll let you know."

Ellie nodded.

"You should probably let the Police and centre management know as well."

"Thank you," Ellie said, "I'll do that."

But first she sped through the rest of the departments, ordering the rest of the goods sent to the collection point as well.

Worrying a little about what the mounting cost of the spree was going to come to, and how long it would take to pay the debt off.

Then to a mobile phone store to buy a new phone, cancel the old one, and get her account transferred across to the new phone.

Called to the locksmith again, made a new booking, resulting in a deadline for getting back home before he arrived.

Eventually found the Centre Management Office up a dark alley with a blown light fixture, to find it closed. She took a picture of the contact details on the door to call them later.

All done, she queued for a taxi from the stand to the Porterfield collection point and back home.

Got her shopping up the stairs in just two heavily laden trips.

The last, with help from the locksmith.

"Bad luck getting your bag stolen the same day your flat got broken into," he said.

She didn't disagree, but wasn't entirely sure luck had anything to do with it.

"Good luck for you, though," she replied.

He grunted and gave her a discount. Maybe he'd noticed her mismatched shoes as well.

Back inside, shoes and coat off, with the door locked and dead-bolted, she put a load of smalls on to wash, then unpacked the television and plugged it in. Scrolled through the menus to let it tune itself.

As the television searched for channels, it alternately crackled with static and blared with talking, so she muted it.

Then put a saucepan of thick chicken and sweetcorn soup on the stove.

Refilled the sink, washed the new crockery and glass-ware, filling up even more garbage bags and leaving them by the door.

Opened a bottle of dry, crisp Pinot Grigio and poured herself a very generous glassful. Half of which she drank in one swallow.

Taking the drive from her pocket, she turned it over and over, looking for something distinctive about it. Absently tapping it on the counter between turns as she leaned on the counter sipping the wine.

Was it possible the guy from the morning's bus stop in-cident had slipped it into her bag without her noticing?

Her own thoughts had consumed her, leaving her obliv-ious to her surroundings. Noticing nothing, let alone any-thing suspicious, before he'd bowled her over.

Why the bag and not the pocket? Or were her hands in the pockets?

Wouldn't the bag have been more complicated? Or was he a reverse pickpocket?

And if it was him, was he a bad guy or a good guy?

If he was the good guy, did that make the guy who broke into her apartment a bad guy.

She was pretty sure good guys didn't break into other people's apartments and leave all their food and clothes out on the floor.

Least ways, according to the movies, not unless the stakes were sky high and there was no time to ask politely.

Were the stakes high?

Not if you watched the news. No suggestion of anything untoward. But if the stakes were that high, "they" wouldn't risk mass panic would they?

As a teenager in care, she didn't have a computer of her own, just as shared one in the common room that was always monopolised by the gamers.

And not being a gamer, she hadn't bothered to get one when she'd got her own place.

By the time she'd thought it might be a good idea, she'd got a smart phone and didn't think a seperate computer was worth the cost.

Which meant she couldn't see what was on the drive.

Though maybe it would work on her tablet.

And now she thought about it, where was her tablet? She didn't remember seeing it, and it wasn't on the shelf where she usually kept it.

Had the burglar taken it?

Probably.

Just as well; given her luck that day, if she'd tried to plug the drive into the tablet it would've blown up, taking her and the apartment with it.

So what to do with the drive?

Turn it into the Police?

She hadn't reported her bag stolen at that point, but wanted to wait until she could decide the best way to mention someone'd added a flash drive to it.

Or maybe it would be better to throw it in the bin and pretend she'd never seen it?

Her knowledge of movie spies suggested she would end up dead if she didn't have it to bargain with.

But if she kept it, where could she hide it?

She was in no doubt that whoever broke in the first time would have no trouble getting in, let alone trashing the place a second time.

The sound of rapidly boiling soup recalled her to the moment, and she dropped the drive in her haste to turn the soup off.

As she was trying to get the contents of the hot pan into a bowl after half a large glass of wine on an empty stomach and a very trying day when she heard a large thud and looked up to see the door flying across the apartment towards her.

Leaving a trail of hot soup over the counter and her foot as she started hopping and trying to set the pan down on a trivet on the counter at the same time.

A task that suddenly seemed unimportant as the door barely slowed as it pushed the dresser around and smashed it into the kitchenette, halting both their progress.

She looked up at the gargantuan black suited man who had to duck and turn sideways through the doorway to get into the apartment.

Her mouth fell open as she set her foot down and dropped the hot pan on it. Barely noticing the soup scalding her feet as the man loomed over her.

"Where's the drive?" he demanded in a gravelly voice.

Ellie couldn't say anything. Her brain had shut the critical thinking function down.

She giggled. The locksmith had been right; one good kick was all it took to bring the door down.

He put both his hands on her shoulder and shook her, "where's the drive?"

She giggled again, brain locked in on the way the door had flown across the room.

Now she had to call the property agent back to tell them a man whose size defied comprehension had kicked the door in.

He lost patience and slapped her face with the back of his hand, sending her spinning out of his grip and landing with a crunch she barely felt before losing consciousness.

7

When Ellie came to, she was not in her apartment.

And given the day she'd had, not shocked to be tied to a chair in what sounded like a small dark room.

On her own.

Just like the best traditional crime movies.

Struggling to free herself, she realised she was bound with a something like plastic cable ties, so her chances of escape were minimal.

And the chair was a plastic picnic chair; rigid enough not to collapse, but still too flexible to get a precarious balance on two legs.

As she wrestled to get free, it felt more like the legs would bend than break.

On the bright side, she didn't have a bag over her head. She could breathe easily, and the air was reasonably fresh.

The ambient temperature was comfortable enough given she was still wearing the track pants and a t-shirt, though she felt the hint of a breeze across her bare arms, possibly from an open or cracked window.

Her feet were bare against a carpeted floor. The type of cheap but durable carpet that comes in tiles you glue to the floor of storage or lunch rooms in manufacturing facilities.

Now she was thinking about her feet, she could feel the burns.

And what must surely be a faceful of bruise, with a large lump or cut on her temple.

Ignoring a twinge of pain, she tilted her head to listen, hearing indistinct voices, perhaps foreign, some distance away. In another room, no, a corridor, and they were walking down towards her.

The situation was so far out of her experience, she couldn't help imagining a small subtitle banner saying "indistinct voices, perhaps foreign," across the floor.

She opened her eyes a crack, to see a plain room meagrely lit by a light shining from behind her.

No one in front of her, just stuffed shelves and cupboards as far as she could see without turning her head.

She risked turning her head to the right to see a window behind her, just below roof height, through which something like a street light shone, and a large cloth covered thing that could have been a pool table or a stack of crates of contraband.

A basement?

Twisting her head to the left, she saw a door opposite the window.

Okay, sensible, she guessed.

Turn the kidnap victim's chair away from the door.

But the fact of not being able to see what might happen behind her made her skin crawl.

So, she was in something like a storage room, maybe on an abandoned property.

With some species of goons outside.

Or indentured workers under duress.

Hopefully not a locked up storage facility with people about to lock up and leave her behind.

She wondered what her chances of a bathroom break were.

Also minimal, she deduced.

She considered the progress of her evening so far:

Apartment broken into.

Bag stolen.

Apartment broken into again.

Kidnapped.

Completely out of the ordinary.

And the other thing completely out of the ordinary she'd been through that day was a guy collapsing on top of her at the bus stop.

It seemed highly likely that everything else had all happened because of him.

She couldn't come up with any other explanation.

And given the circumstances of her arrival wherever she was now, she had to conclude that he was the good guy.

Because movie good guys never slap the crap out of women, and bad guys do.

Or if not women, then dogs, cats or other creatures of the companion variety.

So had Bus Stop Guy stolen the drive from them, or was he trying to keep it out of their hands?

Not that it mattered.

She was here; she didn't know where the drive was, and he was in a hospital somewhere else entirely.

With no way to contact him, even if she knew who he was.

But she remembered the feel of his cheap suit beneath her fingers.

Maybe he was a whistle-blower, and she was a hero for helping him escape.

Which still didn't help her.

Bad guys don't care who they hurt.

Ellie struggled with her bonds again, wondering if they were less tight, or it was her imagination.

Out of curiosity, she rocked the chair backwards and forwards, then side to side, hoping to overturn it like they did in the movies.

She wasn't much good at it, not weighing enough to tip the flexible chair enough to make it move significantly, but somehow, the ties loosened a little more.

Stifling a moan, she struggled with the ties and got an ankle loose. Redoubling her efforts, she released her arms as well, pulling them in front of her, marvelling at the cuts she'd barely noticed in her desperation to get free.

She bent over, intending to free her foot, but finally overbalanced and unintentionally landed face first on the carpet.

Adding a carpet burn to her list of injuries.

Stifling a grunt of pain.

Pulling at the tie with her hands while she levered it with her ankle, at last setting her other ankle free.

Looking at the blood, she felt sick for a moment, and curled into the foetal position. Placing her hands over her heart, hoping to calm it.

Did the carpeted floor suggest she was in someone's house?

Though it didn't actually rule out being left for dead in a secure storage locker.

Ellie couldn't seem to catch a breath.

The blood roared in her ears and she felt dizzy.

Though maybe that was just the blood circulating back through her hands and feet once more.

Knowing she was hyperventilating, she forced herself to close her eyes again and take a deep breath.

Several times, until she kept a lungful in for a count of ten wild heartbeats.

As she lay on the floor counting her heartbeats, she flicked through her mental movie filing cabinet, and realised many of the happy endings directly resulted from concerned friends and family calling the authorities.

If she was somewhere at the terminal end of the spectrum, she was well and truly on her own.

Liam Neeson was not coming to rescue her.

Holding her legs to her torso while she wiggled her toes, she resolved to join a club or dating app or something and get to know more people once she got clear of all this mess.

And get the door to her apartment fixed properly.

So, if no one was coming for her, she had to rescue herself. If she didn't rescue, she'd probably end up on the cutting room floor.

Literally.

"Then let's get a bloody move on before they come back," she said.

Pressing her lips together, and ignoring the pain in her feet, she climbed upright and carried the chair to the window.

Placing the chair precisely, she gave it a good shove to make sure she hadn't damaged it during the effort of freeing herself, and reassured, stepped up on it to look at the window.

It was an unlocked sliding window.

And when she opened it fully, a gust of cold air blew in, making her shiver.

Outside it was full night, though a fancy imitation period street lamp illuminated a concrete path half overgrown by a bunch of bushes.

It was looking more like a house, but that didn't rule out a storage locker.

Then again, going by the pale sandstone cladding of the building, perhaps it was a genuine period street lamp.

No guards, so she popped the fly-screen.

It clattered to the ground, and she waited for someone to shout or come running, but all was quiet.

She was afraid of what she might find if she climbed out, but more afraid of what might happen if she stayed inside the room.

She scrubbed her face with her hands and ran her fingers through her hair.

Despite the sinking feeling in her guts, she took another deep, bolstering breath, and jumped up, hauling herself to the edge of the window and crawled out.

Flopping on the damp concrete, giving her arms a minute to rest.

Grinning as she savoured the fact of her escape from the room.

Then flinching as a gust of wind pushed some twigs along the path towards her.

She had to move.

The cold was biting, especially on her bare feet and arms. As if the path was draining the warmth out of her body.

She looked around, trying to decide whether following the path was a better option than going bush.

If they had cameras, she reasoned, most likely they'd be infra-red and able to see her in the dark regardless of which way she went.

If she stuck to the path, at least she'd be able to see where she was going.

And minimise further pain and bodily injury.

She crouched as she trotted along the path, and it wasn't long before she came to a corner of the building.

Her side was stone, and the other brick, which probably meant she was approaching the service side of the building.

The service side was more brightly lit than the other, with a loading bay across the back. The concrete path ended in a bitumen area that looked to be half drive widening out to the loading bay with an open space on the other side for vehicles to park.

Currently empty.

No cars, vans, people (gun wielding or not), or dogs.

A grass boundary followed the edge of the drive, and on the assumption it would hurt her feet less than the bitumen, she started running along the grass.

Listening, hearing nothing but her labouring breath.

Not looking back until her pathetic body couldn't run anymore.

No shouting, no searchlights, no people pouring from the building like ants.

No obvious sign of pursuit at all.

She started walking again, hugging herself and hoping at some point the drive would come to a road where she could lose any pursuers.

While figuring out where she was, and how to get home when she didn't have any money or identification.

A while later, the drive ended at a road.

Still no signs of pursuit.

She took a moment to look up at the sign, which explained everything.

A well-known self-storage company.

Impossibly, her blood ran colder than it already was.

Had they planned to just lock her in and leave her there?

Imagining for a moment, the storage company auctioning off the right to break into the locker in a few years when they stopped paying the storage fee.

And found her dessicated body there.

She shivered, not entirely from the cold.

Still with no idea where she was, and fairly confident no one was after her, she turned left because she didn't have to cross the drive and blindly followed the road.

Grappling being alone in a storage locker. How would it have taken her to die?

She'd watched a documentary a while back, which had said about three days.

Probably less, given she'd eaten nothing and only drunk a glass of wine.

Would the locker be hot during the day, making her sweat more? Would she be colder at night if bathed in salt from sweat?

Or would she just pass out or fall asleep and die when her fluid level got too low to maintain her blood pressure?

Would it hurt?

She realised her footsteps had slowed to a stop, and that she couldn't feel her feet.

She had to stop the negative thoughts and get a move on.

But she was shivering so much she stumbled on a seam in the concrete path, pausing to look at it, trying to work out what it was.

She knew there was something very important she needed to do, but she couldn't remember what it was.

"Are you okay?"

She looked up to see a long-haired blonde guy hanging out of a soft-serve ice-cream van, and stumbled over to the van, dreamily leaning into the window glass, reading the menu inside.

"Choc-vanilla," she said.

"I really don't think you're okay," he said.

Ellie looked behind her, "choc-vanilla Mum! I want choc-vanilla."

The guy got out of the van and reached out a hand to touch her arm. "You're frozen!" he said, and pulled the fleece off his body.

Pulling it over her head and down her body, layering her with the warmth of his body.

He opened the passenger side door and lifted her in, folding the seatbelt around her, before shutting the door.

Ellie felt she should have been concerned about this, but couldn't call to mind why.

All she knew for sure was she was warmer and out of the wind.

8

Ellie woke in a single room in a hospital.

She knew it was a hospital, because she was wearing a hospital gown, connected up to a drip, and had one of those prong things up her nose.

There was a machine that beeped periodically, and a small monitor rested on her index finger.

All the give-away signs she'd seen in movies.

The room was lit with the dim blueish glow of fluorescent tubes hanging from the ceiling, with one window to her right, looking out over a night sky.

On the left, a waist height cupboard with a telephone resting on the flat surface, and a taller cupboard next to it.

The nose thing was uncomfortable, so she pulled it down.

And her feet hurt, so she lifted the covers to see them heavily bandaged.

A nurse walked through the door, comfortingly wearing a tunic with the hospital's name on it.

"Good, you're awake. Let me take some observations, then I'll get the doctor to speak with you?"

She started by holding something like a space-age gun close to Ellie's forehead. "Temperature thirty seven point eight, so that's good. Looks like the fever's broken and the antibiotics are working."

The nurse put the gun in her pocket, pulled out a slip of paper and a pen, and wrote something down.

Put them back in the pocket and pulled a cuff from somewhere behind Ellie's head before folding it around her arm. Fiddled with something behind Ellie's head and the cuff started inflating.

Ellie jumped, both at the noise and the sensation against her arm

"Don't panic," the nurse said, "it's just going to inflate for a moment and then release."

"It hurts," Ellie said in a small voice.

"Just for an instant," the nurse replied. And it deflated, "one thirty on eighty," she said, "that's good," whipping the cuff off and away.

"Can I get you anything while you wait for the doctor?"

Ellie sat up, clasping her hands. "Hot chocolate?"

The nurse smiled, "I'll see what I can do."

The nurse patted her hand, "do you need me to help you visit the bathroom?"

And as soon as the nurse said it, Ellie needed to go, "please."

The nurse took the nose thing off, helped her out of bed, and dragged the drip pole with her across to a small room inside the bigger room she hadn't noticed until then.

The white-tiled floor, white china sink and toilet reminded Ellie of some place, but she couldn't get a grip on the memory and it floated away.

As she washed her hands, she saw someone with a bandaged head and beaten up face in the mirror and assumed it was another patient standing behind her.

The nurse who helped her back to bed was the first nurse, and as Ellie flopped back, the nurse put the nose thing back in. "please try to leave the nasal cannula in there a little longer."

Ellie nodded hesitantly, knowing it was bad to lie, and knowing she was going to take it off as soon as the nurse had left the room.

But the nurse left her exhausted by the brief excursion, and she soon fell asleep.

9

When Ellie woke again, a lady wearing one of those heart hearing things around her neck was standing at the end of the bed, writing something down in a folder.

"Back again, are we?"

Ellie nodded.

The woman approached, pulling a little torch from her pocket. "May I?"

Ellie nodded again, not sure what she was agreeing to, startled when the woman flashed it in her eyes.

"And listen to your chest?"

Ellie nodded again. The woman rubbed the heart thing on her own chest, "my stethoscope is going to feel a little cold, so I'm just trying to warm it up. Can you sit up and lean forward?"

She put the earplugs in her ears and listened as she moved it around Ellie's back.

"Can you tell me your name?"

"I'm a big girl, of course I know my name, it's...

"It's...

"My name is..."

Ellie burst into tears, "I can't remember my name."

The woman patted her hand and passed over a tissue. Ellie allowed herself to be comforted and blew her nose.

"Can you tell me how old you are?"

Ellie held out her fist and counted out her fingers as she opened it up, "I'm one, two, three, four, five!"

"Are you?" the woman asked, "that's quite grown up isn't it."

"Yes, it is."

"Do you know your address?"

"One, two, three, two Daffodil Road."

The woman leaned in, "do you know how you got to hospital?"

Ellie frowned. And shook her head.

"Where's my mum?"

"She's not here right now, but if you can be very brave for me, I'll call her now."

Ellie blew her nose again and nodded.

"Oh look, here's Nurse Janine with your hot chocolate!"

Ellie clapped her hands and bounced in the bed.

"Shall I put the television on for you while you wait?'

Ellie nodded again, and the woman turned the television on.

"Cartoons!" Ellie said, "my favourite!"

The woman smiled, then the two women left.

10

Sometime later, another lady wheeled a table holding a tray into the room, "here's some breakfast," she said.

Ellie glanced at the window to see the sky lightening.

"Thank you."

The woman dragged the table to the bed, and adjusted the position across the bed.

"Do you know when my Mum's coming."

"I'm sorry, I don't," she said as she was leaving, "but I'm sure it won't be much longer."

Ellie knew it was bad to waste food, so she ate every single bite from the tray; the claggy porridge, the cold toast with margarine and red jam, to the box of orange juice, even diluting the coffee and sugar packets in the hot water and stirring it up with the tea bag.

Right down to licking out the margarine and jam containers.

Then she watched cartoons some more.

Until her eyelids dropped and she fell asleep.

11

When Ellie woke again, light from the window spilled into the room

A man wearing a black suit was in her room, leaning on the wall.

Ellie pulled the blanket up to her chin and drew her knees up underneath it.

The hairs on her arms lifted.

She held her breath, conducting her own inventory as he looked at her.

He had the same black hair as her.

The same square face.

And his eyes were blue like hers too.

She lowered the blanket slightly.

"Do you know me Melissa?" he asked.

She shook her head.

"I'm your father."

"No," she said softly.

Then again louder, "no."

Getting louder and louder until she was screaming, "no, no, no, no, noooo.

"My father is dead."

A couple of nurses ran in as as her voice escalated. "You're not my father, as a nurse ushered him out of the room and another approached her with a needle.

"My father is in heaven waiting for me," she screamed after him, and as the drug hit her system, softer, "he's in heaven...

"Waiting..."

When the drug wore off, it was still daylight, though Ellie wasn't sure whether it was the same day or another day.

Going by the emptiness in her stomach, Ellie thought it must be around lunchtime.

She felt different somehow.

Hollowed out from the inside.

Restless.

A wave of longing almost drowned her, though she wasn't sure what it was she wanted.

Or where it was. How she might get it or why it was so important to her.

During a television commercial promising pest genocide, featuring footage of cartoon insects writhing on their backs, her eyes watered in sympathy.

Was it another blanket she wanted, or a stuffed animal? Maybe a warm hug or a cup of her favourite chicken and sweetcorn soup.

No, it was something bigger than that, something like a house or a place she belonged.

Or her dead mother.

Whatever it was, she knew she was missing something on a fundamental level, and without it, she would never feel whole.

While she was out of it, they had taken the drip from her arm, which was great, though the cannula remained taped to the back of her hand. Which was not so great.

Feeling close to one hundred years old, she hauled herself out of bed and dragged herself to the bathroom.

And sat, trying to understand what it was about the small room that nagged at her.

Having visions of a laundry basket filled with neatly folded washing on the floor next to a front loading washing machine.

And a small drying rack taking up space in the shower cubicle.

Except the bathroom was the wrong way round, though she couldn't say how she knew that.

Flushing the toilet, she looked at her bandaged head and bruised face in the mirror, wincing as she gently touched her face.

Unable to tell whether it actually hurt or she'd just deduced it ought to from what she saw.

She retreated to the bed, leaping onto it as if it were an island, and she had to cross a river with monsters in it. If she wasn't fast enough, the monsters might leap out of the water and catch her. And if they caught her, they'd pull her under the water and eat her drowned and bloated body.

Which was ridiculous because she knew neither the moat nor the monsters existed, even if that weird place of emptiness inside her insisted that a long running jump into the bed was safer than walking across and sitting on it to pull her legs up.

The one time she hadn't run at it, she knew for certain something horrible had happened, but she couldn't remember what. Only knew she couldn't tempt fate again.

She was relieved as she settled her sore feet under the covers, trying to get comfortable.

She was distracted by a small, worn, brown and white stuffed koala bear next to the phone on the cupboard. Something had chewed its leatherette claws down to frills, but it still winked at her with its one brown eye.

She knew how it would feel under her fingers, and what it would smell like when she lifted it to her face, but didn't remember owning it.

Slowly, not completely sure it wasn't a product of her drug fuelled imagination, she leaned over to pick it up.

For a second she remembered owning something very like it, only less threadbare.

She fished a name from somewhere deep and forgotten, "Klala?"

Klala's eye twinkled at her.

He was smaller than she remembered, once he'd been the size of her chest, now less than half.

She lowered her head to sniff the top of his head, smelling the faded scent of lanolin in the wool stuffing.

The smell was soothing, and she snuggled further down the bed, under the covers, tucking it into the hollow between her shoulder and neck, resting her face on it like a pillow.

Ellie turned the television on and flicked to a news channel, hoping she'd see something that might help her make sense of what she was feeling.

Wondering whether a family sized block of chocolate might be better.

And where she could get one.

Then remembering she didn't have any money with her, but remembering her name was Ellie. Even though the hollowness didn't agree.

And the address of her apartment. Where she probably still lived. The apartment with the bathroom that looked a lot like the one in the hospital.

Which left her wondering how she'd ended up in the hospital. Probably walked, given the bandages on her feet and the way they hurt.

Though that didn't explain her swollen face and bandaged head.

It felt like she was missing something important.

"I see you found your bear," a man said.

Startled, she sat up, but relaxed back to the bed when she saw he was tall and thin, with blonde hair, wearing a stethoscope and hospital tunic.

"I'm sorry," he said, "I didn't mean to startle you."

Ellie blushed and smiled.

"How are you feeling?"

"Okay."

He took a temperature gun out of a pocket, "may I?" he asked, and she nodded.

He sat on the edge of the bed and took her temperature.

"Do you mean okay as in better, or okay meaning you have pain but are not complaining because you don't want to bother anyone?"

He swapped the thermometer for a torch, raising an eyebrow at her.

She nodded, and he flashed it in her eyes a couple of times.

"Okay. Not better as such, but the pain is within acceptable parameters."

"And when you say acceptable parameters, how would you score it on a scale of one to ten, if one is not much and ten is you think you're about to die?"

"Hmmm, about a six."

"Okay, but if it gets to seven, let me know and I'll give you something for it."

Ellie protested, but he cut her off, "you'll heal faster and more completely if you keep the pain under control."

Ellie nodded again.

"I heard a story from the man who was in your room earlier today. Are you interested in hearing it?"

"No," Ellie snapped.

He wrapped a blood pressure cuff around her arm and set it off.

"You sure?"

"Yes," Ellie said doubtfully.

As the cuff deflated he said, "it's very sad."

Ellie grunted non-committally, and he stood up.

"Well, if you change your mind, let me know," he said, as he plumped the pillow and smoothed the covers.

He turned away.

"Wait!"

He looked back.

"Tell me the story."

He sat back down.

"Once upon a time, a long time ago, there was a man who ran a shop. He was very much in love with his beautiful wife Ellie, and beautiful daughter called Melissa, and they all lived together in a lovely big house.

"One day he came home to find his house burgled, his wife dead, and his daughter replaced by a ransom note on the kitchen bench. To say he was devastated was an understatement."

Ellie nodded.

"He called the Police, and against their advice, paid the ransom. When the kidnappers didn't give Melissa back, he offered a million dollar reward for information leading to her recovery. When the Police ran out of leads, he hired a private investigator."

Ellie made a small noise of sympathy.

"I told you it was sad."

So, what happened next?"

"Ah, as it turns out, the man was brilliant. Rather than selling the house and moving on as his friends and family suggested, he continued to live in it, because he knew one day his daughter would walk back in the door."

He leaned towards Ellie, and continued at such a low volume she had to lean in to hear him properly, "then one day, this very hospital where you're staying got the number of the house and rang the man and told him there was a woman here who had lost her memory but claimed that she lived at his address!"

Ellie leaned back in the bed, stomach tied in knots. Emotions warring within her.

"I don't remember."

"Sometimes," he said, leaning away again, and speaking at a more natural level, "when you get a blow to the head, you can lose your memories."

Ellie looked at him.

"Sometimes they come back in drips and drabs over the space of a few days or weeks. Sometimes they come back suddenly, all in one go. But sometimes, the circumstances are so dreadful, it seems they've gone forever."

Ellie considered the situation. He hadn't said so, but she knew he was talking about her.

He waited for her to say something.

"I don't remember much. But I remember there was a man in a black suit who I'd never seen before who picked me up from school. Or I suppose at that age, more likely Kinder. He said my parents were dead and took me away to a place I thought was a prison. He said one of my relatives would come pick me up later."

She screwed her face up. "Looking back, I suppose it was a black market adoption agency. I'd get sent away to stay with other people, but I was afraid my family wouldn't find me, so I acted up and got sent back to the prison."

Ellie rubbed tears away from her eyes, and the man patted the leg closest to him.

"We used to play hide and seek," she continued, "I suppose it was practise for the raids, but one time, when I was about ten, I refused to play, and started screaming the place down."

The man patted her leg again, slow comforting pats.

"Some people in uniforms took us away to another place, which was more like a boarding school than a prison, but wasn't actually much better."

She waited for the memory of the time to come crashing back, and it didn't.

But something in the emptiness shifted.

She clasped Klala to her chest.

"What was his name? The man who left Klala?"

"Victor Porterfield."

Ellie nodded.

It didn't rouse any stronger feelings than the name Melissa.

Though it explained her early obsession with the Porterfields.

"You said he has a shop?"

"Well, it's not entirely his. He's one of the Department Store Porterfields.

Ellie smiled with one side of her mouth, "when I was a kid I waited for the Porterfields to come get me. But as I grew older, I convinced myself it was just a coincidence we shared a name."

The man nodded. "I'd say you have a lot to think about, so I'll check in on you before I leave for the day."

"Okay," Ellie said.

"Now then, how's that pain? Still within acceptable parameters?" he said with a smile.

Ellie wanted to lie for the sake of something to put her to sleep and quiet her restless mind, but was afraid if she took anything she'd forget what she'd learned.

"I'm good," she said.

He nodded and left her to her thoughts.

13

How hilarious after all this time, to find out Ellie was, as she'd once thought, one of THE Porterfields.

Which made her wonder who organised her first kidnapping, and whether it was the same person who'd organised the second.

And what they'd done with the money.

Her mother was the only one beyond suspicion, on account of her dying at the scene. Though not even really that.

There was that movie where the woman faked her death to get away from her abusive husband. Which was a movie, but even so. Was Mother really dead, and was she really innocent of the kidnapping?

Or was Mother's plan to take the money and whisk her child away somewhere "safe?" And if the plan had gone wrong, had her lover/accomplice ditched the child/evidence?

Or worse, taken the ransom money and sold the child using his underworld connections.

Though that might have been a step too far.

Had she known something wasn't right? Was that why she'd taken her mother's name instead of her own?

Wasn't it more likely they'd have found her under her own name? Or had her mother told her not to use her name?

Ellie rubbed her temples; the whole thing was making her head ache.

She couldn't even be sure her father was beyond suspicion. Almost the same plan would have worked for him with a few tweaks.

But more likely, one or more of the other Porterfields were behind both kidnappings. She doubted she'd have recognised them, but maybe they'd seen her at the store, and worried she might remember something incriminating.

She needed to know what they looked like, and for the first time, wished she had a computer so she could look them up.

Maybe that was why her tablet was the only thing stolen from the apartment.

Trash the place so she wouldn't notice it was missing.

Was it even possible that Bus Stop Guy and the flash drive had nothing to do with the second kidnapping?

And had Bus Stop Guy given it to her because she was a Porterfield, or was that just random happenstance?

She shuddered at the idea someone had known who she was when she didn't, let alone targeted her because she was a Porterfield after all.

Where even was the flash drive?

She'd been playing with it before The Giant had kicked the door down.

Dropped it, and then what?

Though hadn't The Giant wanted it? Didn't he demand it before he hit her?

Her head throbbed as she tried to force herself to remember.

She put her hands up to her head and squeezed it; partly to make her brain smaller so it didn't hurt, and partly to force the memory out.

And then she remembered her new television had a connection that would take a flash drive.

The sales assistant had said something about using one to take her favourite movies with her wherever she went.

Which had seemed redundant at the time; no place to take movies, and if she was going to watch a movie at home, she'd rent one from the library or use a streaming service.

But if she slipped the drive into the television, she'd probably be able to see the contents, though maybe not open them.

Assuming she still had it.

She needed to get out of the hospital

With a burst of fresh energy, she climbed out of the bed again, and checked the cupboards for her clothes, which were nowhere to be seen.

Which put a bit of a crimp in her plans.

Wouldn't get far in a hospital gown, especially with bandaged feet.

Some kind soul was bound to assume she'd escaped from a mental institution and call the Police to send her back.

Should she call the Police? Maybe if she'd still had the card with Officer Kirpatrick's number on it.

As it was, the idea of explaining everything was exhausting, especially as all she had was suspicion. Nothing they'd call evidence.

Or would the hospital have sent her clothes and scrapings from under her fingernails and combed her hair for particles to go into evidence for a Police investigation on the woman who was obviously a victim of assault and lost her memory?

She needed help.

And as she'd previously identified, while tied to a chair in a storage facility, she had no one to call on.

Except...

Some guy who'd just claimed he was her father.

Who may or may have had something to do with her kidnapping or the murder of her mother.

But, father or not, she needed help.

And if he was the only one...

Could she just ask for it?

But what would she ask for?

She got back into bed to stay warm.

First, she needed clothes. But her clothes were in the apartment, and after the first lunatic burglar touching them, she still needed to wash them all.

Second, unless The Giant had bothered to pick up the door, put it back in place and lock it, someone else had probably stripped her apartment bare by now.

It was possible the agent had got the door fixed, in which case the door was probably unlocked with the new key in the apartment (which didn't seem likely), and stripped bare.

Third, The Giant had retrieved the drive, which may or may not have incriminating evidence on it, and returned to its "rightful" owner, in which case there wasn't much point in checking the apartment for it.

But it was a tiny drive, and could have wound up under a cupboard, or a splash of chicken and sweetcorn soup, or something else, and was possibly still there.

Could she ask her father to check the place out and try to find it?

Which led her back to Porterfields.

The security guards in the store wore black suits. And she'd seen security guards in places like hotels and night clubs wearing black suits, so it didn't seem like too much of a leap to imagine that body guards and other personal security might have black suits as well.

Of course, that didn't mean that either Bus Stop Guy or The Giant worked at Porterfield or were even security guards.

But she couldn't help but think there was a connection between the two.

But how?

So.

Police no. Alleged father, nothing to lose.

She wanted clean clothes and pictures of the Porterfield family. Maybe the senior staff as well.

As for the drive...

She'd wait until she knew whether she still had it.

Ellie fiddled with the television thing until she found the call button for the nurse.

14

A nurse Ellie hadn't seen before arrived.

"Are you okay?" she asked.

"What? Oh. Yes, I'm fine. There was a man who visited me earlier today, and I wonder if you could call him back?"

"Victor? He's still here. Shall I send him in?"

Ellie nodded, "thanks."

Then attempted to neaten herself up a bit.

The man poked his head around the door.

"Look," Ellie said, "I don't remember you, and I'd like to get to know you, but right now I need a favour."

She explained her theory.

It seemed Victor had pre-empted her, bringing a bag of things he hoped would trigger her memories, not just Klala, but photo albums as well.

Ellie flicked through the pictures, looking for something or someone familiar. Pausing now and again to look at her mother, though she didn't recognise the woman in the pictures.

About the time she was ready to give up, she noticed a picture of a young man sitting in a booth with another man. A taller, broader man.

She took the image from the sleeve and brought it closer to her face, mentally adding a couple of decades.

The man looked a lot like one of her recent clients, frowning; she remembered a fitting for a flounced fuchsia tea dress she'd privately thought an appalling dress, and an even worse look for him.

Something slimmer in more of a lavender hue would have suited him better. She hadn't said anything, as he hadn't looked the sort to appreciate the suggestion.

"Who's this?" she asked.

"Cousin Julius, why?"

"He visited the salon oh... few months back."

"Salon?"

"Ah, you wouldn't know. I work at the Porterfield VIP salon."

He spluttered, "for how long?"

Ellie shrugged, "few years."

"I'm in the same building. I can't believe I've never seen you."

"Well... We can talk about that later. Who's this other guy?"

"Julius' husband."

"Then why would he care I saw him at the salon?"

"He's cheating on his husband?" Victor said doubtfully.

Ellie grunted, "I'm pretty sure he's the guy that kicked my door down and kidnapped me."

"I can't believe it!"

"I was wondering whether the same person might be responsible for both my kidnappings."

"It's possible."

Ellie scratched her nose, "are you still in touch with the original detectives?"

"They retired and handed my case over to a woman who calls me once a year to tell me there's nothing new."

They grinned at each other for a minute before getting embarrassed and looking away.

"Why don't you call her and see what she comes back with?"

"I think I will."

15

As it turned out, Julius had been expecting the Police to arrive since he'd first seen Ellie at the salon. He basically collapsed and explained everything.

He'd been living beyond his means, drinking, gambling, having affairs. He'd started embezzling and the files on the stolen drive were the proof.

It was a coincidence the stolen drive had come to her, but once Julius had realised she was working at Porterfield, he knew he had to get rid of Ellie, regardless.

And since Bus Stop Guy had died from his injuries, there was another charge for Julius to answer for.

16

Ellie paused outside the library, admiring the way the red sunset bathed the gardens in a warm orange glow.

She took a deep breath, fighting the hornets in her stomach.

It had been a long, hard road to get to this point, and if she was honest with herself, she was terrified.

More terrified of walking into a room with a group of strangers sharing a potential interest than during the period of the burglary.

Perhaps because she'd had weeks to think about it, getting more nervous as she imagined all the worst-case scenarios she could think of as the days passed.

But in the space of one single day, she'd been the victim of two home break-ins, and her cousin's husband had kidnapped her.

All over and done with before, she'd even really had the time to think about it.

Not to mention discovering her cousin's husband was also responsible for her childhood abduction and ransom. And if that wasn't enough, that her father had paid the ransom, and hadn't seen her again. Luckily, the second kidnapping had uncovered the first.

After all that, how could she possibly be afraid of walking into a library to meet potential new friends at a book club meeting?

She owed it to herself and Bus Stop Guy to go through with it and make friends.

After all, she'd read at least some of the book. And given her own history, the sweeping generational saga of love, loss and betrayal had been hard to swallow.

She would've preferred something with serial killers, but beggars can't be choosers when it comes to making friends.

She squared her shoulders and forced herself to walk up the steps and through the doors.

Then realised she didn't know where to go from there.

Stopped to ask a librarian, "meeting room two," she whispered, pointing at a partially open door across the room.

"Thanks," she whispered back.

Tapped on the door, "Greendale book club?" she asked.

A red-haired and bearded man stood up, "you must be Ellie? I'm Fred," and pointing one by one to the other people in the room, "this is Ulrika, Marcie, Walter, and Eric. We're missing a few this week, but you can meet them next time.

"So tell us, what did you think of the book?"

Ellie blushed, "I didn't like it much, couldn't get past page one hundred and two when Sweetie crashed the plane."

The room erupted into laughter.

"I didn't even get that far," Ulrika said, "couldn't believe Peter would chase his son Stephen out of the house like that."

"You think that's bad," Walter said, "I didn't even get past the first page."

"We usually read mystery," Marcie chortled, "but thought we'd try for a different genre."

Ellie sat down, "thank god this isn't your usual kind of stuff. Have you read the latest Epiphany Bombshell?"

THE END

ABOUT THE AUTHOR

Alexandria Blaelock writes stories, some of them for *Ellery Queen's Mystery Magazine* and *Pulphouse Fiction Magazine.*

She's also written five self-help books applying business techniques to personal matters like getting dressed, cleaning house, and feeding your friends.

Discover more at www.alexandriablaelock.com.

… you might also like Taipan vs Brown.

The Robin Hood of Private Detectives

Georgia Garside. Foul-mouthed Private Investigator. Ex-contortionist.

Out of her depth. In over her head.

Caught up in the war between a wealthy industrialist and the ex-sugar babe who can't take a hint.

A laugh-out-loud tripartite battle of wits, winner takes all.

www.ingramcontent.com/pod-product-compliance
Lightning Source LLC
Chambersburg PA
CBHW030808190726
48285CB00003B/1084